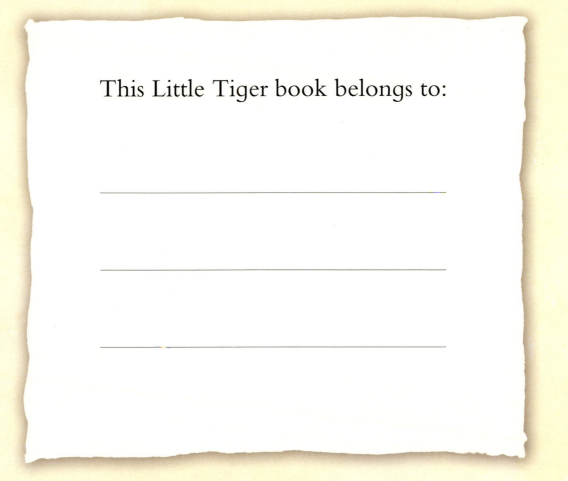

This Little Tiger book belongs to:

_____

_____

_____

Cuddle Bear

Claire Freedman   Gavin Scott

LITTLE TIGER
LONDON

If you feel a little sad,
Or lonely, lost and blue,
Don't worry, call for Cuddle Bear…

...He's always there for you!

Do you need cuddles, cheer-up hugs,
Or snuggle times to share?
Then Cuddle Bear is made for you –
A hug-you-happy bear!

This panda needs a
cuddle NOW!
She's tripped and
had a fright,

So Cuddle Bear

comes scooting up…

A **hug** will put things right.

Poor Penguin's
missing all her friends,
Alone and far away,

But not too far
for Cuddle Bear

To bring a hug –
HOORAY!

The animals are scared of Lion,
He looks so big and wild.

He's **never,**
ever had a hug,
That's why he's
never smiled.

"We all need hugs!" says Cuddle Bear,
"However fierce we look."
Now Lion's happy as can be.
One hug was all it took!

Next Little Rabbit wants a hug,

A happy, bouncy one!

A squishy-squashy-squeezy hug
Is **super** cuddly fun!

It really doesn't matter,
If you're

BIG...

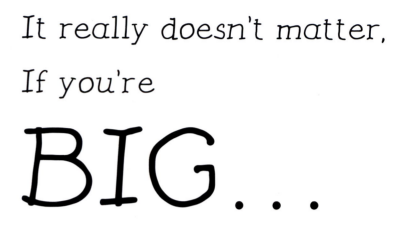

or short...

...or **tall,**

"A hug from me," says Cuddle Bear,
"Will stretch to fit you **all!**"

"The world needs hugs!" says Cuddle Bear,
"To make each day feel bright.
So stretch both arms and wrap them round
Your friends to hug them tight!"

So now you know the secret!
Here's what you have to do...

Just **hug** the person that you love,
And they will **hug you, too!**

For Mr Cuddles – my very own Cuddle Bear! – C F

For Little Elise, with love xx – G S

LITTLE TIGER PRESS LTD,
an imprint of the Little Tiger Group
1 Coda Studios, 189 Munster Road, London SW6 6AW
www.littletiger.co.uk

First published in Great Britain 2012
This edition published 2020
Text copyright © Claire Freedman 2012 • Illustrations copyright © Gavin Scott 2012
Claire Freedman and Gavin Scott have asserted their rights to be identified
as the author and illustrator of this work under the Copyright,
Designs and Patents Act, 1988
A CIP catalogue record for this book is available from the British Library

ISBN 978-1-78881-796-7
Printed in China
LTP/1800/3240/0320
2 4 6 8 10 9 7 5 3 1